Dirtballs

Jada Cooper

First Edition

PAGE PUBLISHING, INC.
New York, NY

First originally published by Page Publishing, Inc. 2019

ISBN 978-1-64424-957-4 (Paperback)
ISBN 978-1-64424-961-1 (Digital)

Printed in the United States of America

For my family, the best people I know. I'm so thankful God blessed me with such a loving family. I've come to realize that there is nothing more valuable on this earth than the people you love and the people who love you.

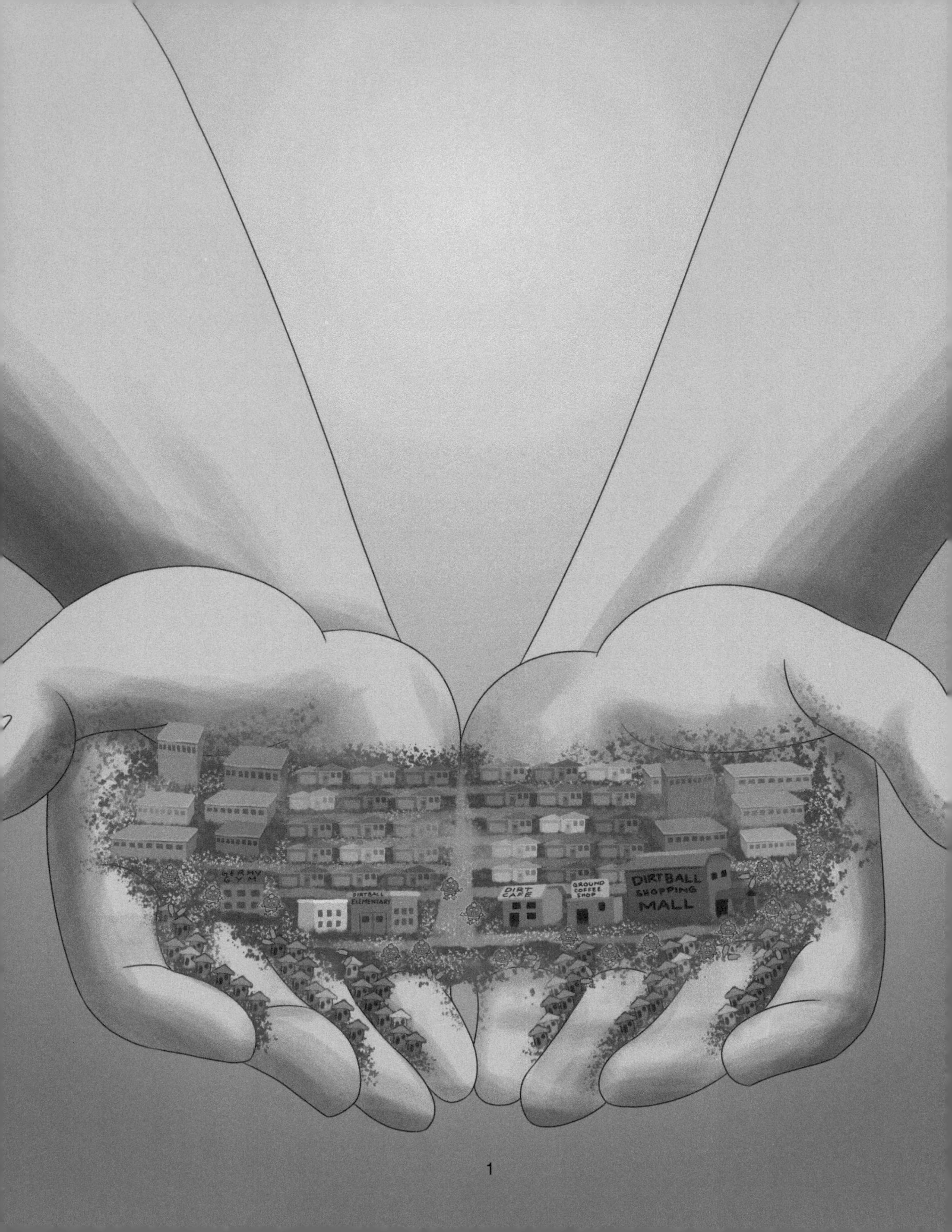
GERMY GYM
DIRTBALL ELEMENTARY
DIRT CAFE
GROUND COFFEE SHOP
DIRTBALL SHOPPING MALL

Don't forget to wash your hands or dirtballs will make long-term plans. They'll take over and set up shop. Unless you wash, they just won't stop! Their town is filled with trash and junk; their neighborhood smells like a skunk!

They'll build tall buildings, shopping malls, germy gyms with climbing walls, coffee shops, and a Dirt Café where they'll make mud pies every day.

DIRT CAFE
MENU
MUDDIES
DIRT LATTES
MUD SHAKES
GROUND COFFEE
MUD CAKE
DIRT TIMES

They'll build houses, tennis courts, and play all sorts of germy sports. They'll even build a germy school; they'll multiply and that's not cool!

Dirtballs are so very icky; some are slimy, some are sticky! These weird brown bugs with bushy tails are hiding underneath your nails.

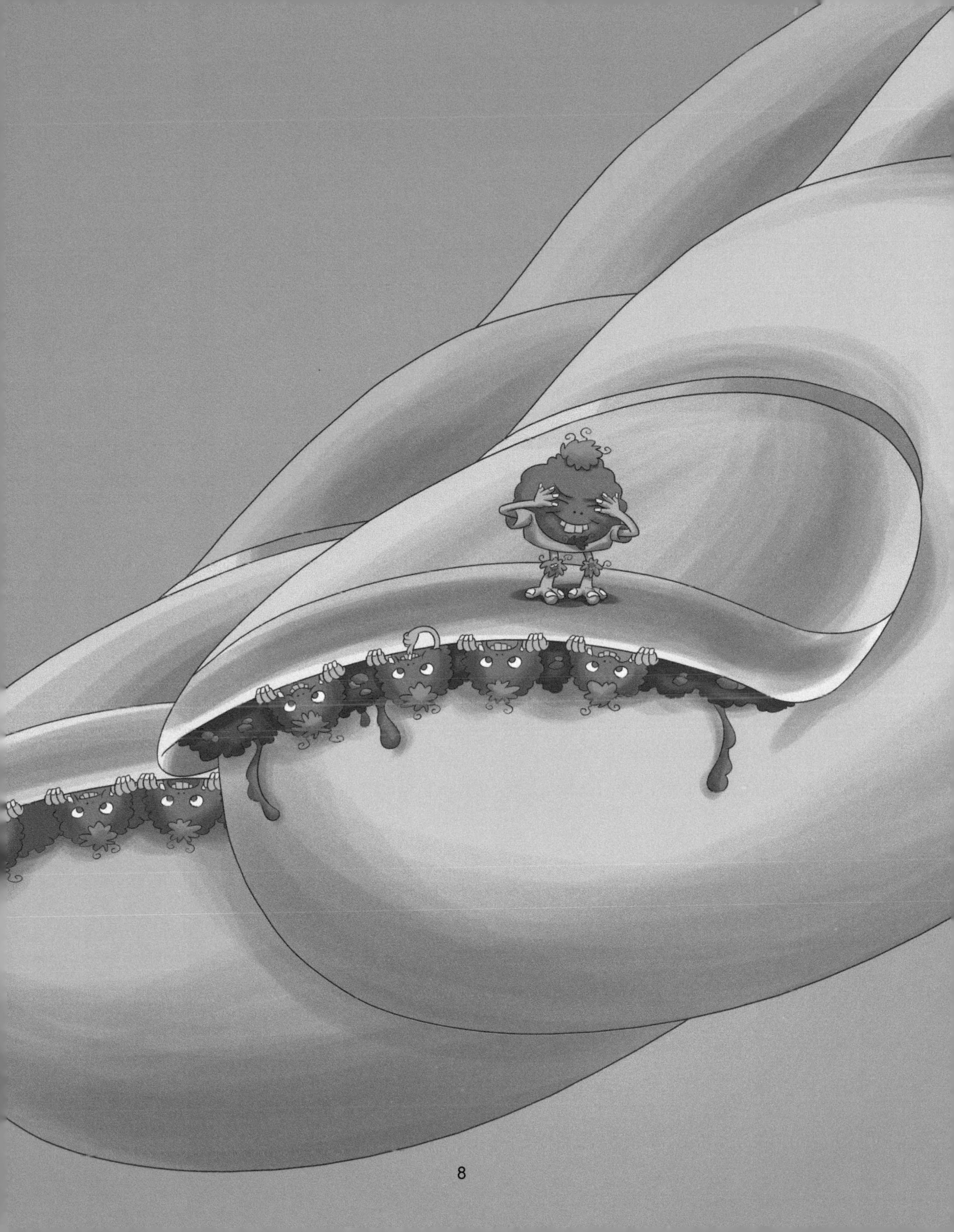

FLEA PARK

Dirtballs smell like rotten eggs! They have long toenails and chicken legs. The weirdest part is their hairy knees where they keep all their pet fleas.

Their noses are slimy and always snotty; they always forget to flush the potty! They have bad manners and always act crusty. Their teeth are best described as rusty.

TOYS
TOILET
TOYS
FORGOT TO FLUSH AGAIN

When dirtballs eat, they show their food; they slurp and chomp and act so rude. They always chew their fingernails and spit them on each other's tails.

Dirtballs think it's nice to stare, and they never wash their greasy hair! They all jump rope with their earwax and brush the hair on each other's backs.

DIRTBALL ELEMENTARY

They never cover when they sneeze, just let their snot blow in the breeze! In the wintertime, they build dirt snowmen and have dirtball fights with their dirtball friends.

Their homes are made of mud and sand; their whole town is on your hand. Your fingers are like little streets to these nasty bugs with three-toed feet!

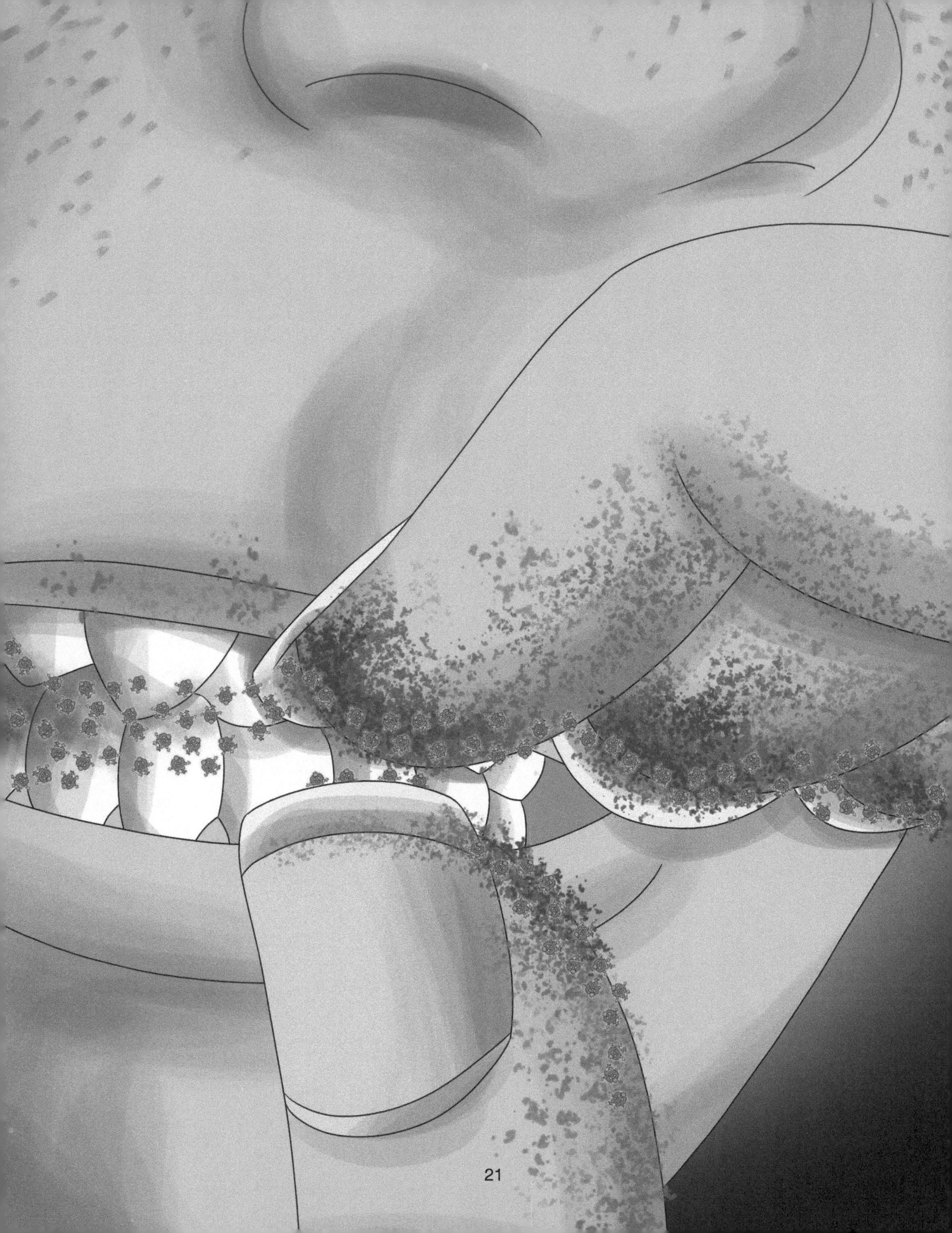

Remember, if you bite your nails, you're eating bugs with bushy tails! Don't do that for goodness' sake or you might get a bellyache!

Scrub your hands before each meal.
You can't see germs but they are real!
Before breakfast, lunch, and dinner,
wash your hands and be a winner!

After the bathroom, please don't forget; those are the grossest of all bugs yet. Picture them as stinky and scary—big, sharp teeth, and very hairy!

You don't want germs on your plate; soap and water just can't wait! Scrub your hands and don't be smug. No one wants to eat a bug!

About the Author

Jada Cooper, the author of *Butter Teeth* and now *Dirtballs*, inspires kids to have healthier habits through imagination and humor. She lives in Alabama with her husband, Jeremiah, and her two sons, Brody and Maddox.

CPSIA information can be obtained
at www.ICGtesting.com
Printed in the USA
BVHW021050180322
631854BV00018B/48